1-

CHOOSE-YOUR-FATE ADVENTURE BOOK

SUPERMAN™

Peace in the Balance

Michael Teitelbaum

Superman created by
Jerry Siegel and Joe Shuster

STARSCAPE

A Tom Doherty Associates Book
New York

This is a work of fiction. All of the characters, organizations, and events portrayed in this novel are either products of the author's imagination or are used fictitiously.

SUPERMAN: PEACE IN THE BALANCE:
CHOOSE-YOUR-FATE ADVENTURE BOOK

Copyright © 2013 by DC Comics.
SUPERMAN and all related characters and elements are trademarks of and © DC Comics.
WB SHIELD: ™ & © Warner Bros. Entertainment Inc.
(s13)

A Starscape Book
Published by Tom Doherty Associates, LLC
175 Fifth Avenue
New York, NY 10010

www.tor-forge.com

ISBN 978-0-7653-6480-7

Starscape books may be purchased for educational, business, or promotional use. For information on bulk purchases, please contact Macmillan Corporate and Premium Sales Department at 1-800-221-7945 extension 5442 or write specialmarkets@macmillan.com.

First Edition: May 2013

Printed in the United States of America

0 9 8 7 6 5 4 3 2 1

How to Read this Book

You are Superman. You control your own destiny in the story you are about to read. How? At the end of each chapter, you will be asked to make a choice about what you do next. In some chapters, you will be asked to solve a puzzle that will provide a clue to help you make your choice. Occasionally you will come to a chapter that closes with "THE END." When that happens, you can go back to the beginning of the book and start again, making different choices, resulting in different outcomes.

Remember, whatever happens in the story happens because of the choices you make. So choose wisely, and get ready for the adventure of a lifetime... or *two*...or *ten*...or *twenty*!

1

YOU are Superman. You are also Clark Kent.

As Clark, you have just arrived at the office of your editor, Perry White at the *Daily Planet*. You stand by the door waiting as Perry paces back and forth screaming into the phone.

"How should I know who let the dogs out?" he yells. "Do I look like the Metropolis Dogcatcher? I don't know. Call the shelter!"

Perry slams down the phone, then looks up and notices you.

"Kent!" Perry blusters. "Sit down! I have here what could be the most important assignment of your career."

Uh-huh, you think, smiling to yourself. *Perry says the same thing every time he assigns me a story.*

"Kent, are you listening?" Perry yells.

"Of course, Mr. White," you reply, setting up a new document in your laptop computer. "I'm all ears."

"OK, then," Perry grumbles. "The World Peace Conference is starting today. As you know, it's an attempt to solve the world's many conflicts. This conference is being held on an orbiting space station so there is no host country; instead, all countries can work together. And the conference is being attended by the President and the leaders of all the other participating countries."

You type furiously, taking notes.

"By meeting in space, all the delegates can symbolically see the Earth as a unified whole during their attempts to establish peace," Perry continues. "I want you, Kent, on that space station, covering every minute of that Peace Conference. I don't have to say that this could be the most important assignment of your career."

"You already said that, Mr. White," you reply.

"What? Oh yeah," Perry says, shrugging. "Don't be a wise guy, Kent. The whole world will be riveted to your every word to learn about any progress at the Peace Conference. I want you to dig deep, to cover every angle, every meeting, everything of significance that is said on the space station. Even—"

At that moment Jimmy Olsen bursts into Perry White's office.

"Olsen!" Perry barks. "How many times have I told you not to interrupt me when—"

"I'm sorry, Mr. White," Jimmy says.

"You just did it again!" Perry shouts.

"I'm sorry, Mr. White," Jimmy repeats.

"We just got a report that an android has appeared in Washington D.C. and is demanding a meeting with the President!" Jimmy explains.

Your eyes open wide. *An android,* you think. *In D.C.? What in the world could be going on?*

Your impulse is to change into Superman and zoom off to Washington. But you need to get up to the space station for the World Peace Conference.

WHAT SHOULD YOU DO?

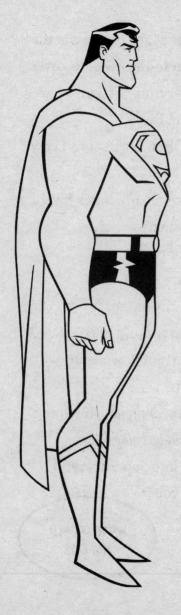

→ If you continue with your plan to go to the space station to cover the Peace Conference, go to 32.

→ If you decide to go to Washington as Superman instead, go to 55.

2

Hoping to gain an edge in deep space combat, you grab Zod and muster all your remaining strength to fly up off the moon and out into space. With the moon no longer blocking the sun's rays, your full power returns—but so does Zod's.

Your titanic struggle continues.

Zod grabs a passing asteroid and slams it into you. The rock shatters into space rubble. At that moment, your super-hearing picks up strange radio waves from Earth.

Am I hearing this correctly? I don't believe this!

→ If you recognize the frequencies, go to 43.

→ If you decide to continue your battle in space, go to 4.

SOLVE THE PUZZLE ON THE NEXT PAGE TO FIGURE OUT YOUR NEXT MOVE.

Code Key

!=A, @=B, #=C, \$=D,
%=E, ^=F, &=G, *=H,
Ω=I, ∑=J, +=K, [=L,
{=M,]=N, }=O, >=P,
<=Q, ?=R, ¢=S, £=T,
¤=U, §=V, Δ=W, ©=X,
€=Y, ◊=Z

SECRET CODE

*Use this Code Key
to decode this secret
coded message:*

@ ? ! Ω] Ω ! #   Ω ¢

@ ! # +   }]   % ! ? £ *

3

There is only one thing that can stop Zod—Kryptonite! But, of course, it can also kill me.

And I know exactly where I can find a chunk of Kryptonite that could do in Zod with only a small risk of causing me any harm.

Got to hurry!

→ If you decide to try to stop Brainiac, go to 35.

→ If you try to stop Zod, go to 20.

SOLVE THE PUZZLE ON THE NEXT PAGE TO FIGURE OUT YOUR NEXT MOVE.

MAZE

4

This battle with Zod is too evenly matched. It could go on forever. I've got to investigate what's happening back on Earth. I don't know how it happened, but apparently, Brainiac 2.5 has returned.

And so, even though you hate to do it, you break free of Zod and speed back to Earth.

"You cannot escape me by running away, Kal-El!" Zod snarls. "I will follow you to the ends of the universe and then destroy you!"

True to his word, Zod follows you, right on your heels, all the way back to Earth.

Within seconds you are back on Earth. Your super-hearing traces the radio signal to Tokyo. Flying to Japan, you discover Brainiac 2.5 flinging Omega Spears at random. Windows shatter and buildings crumble as people panic and flee in every direction.

You attack Brainiac 2.5, dodging a flurry of his Omega Spears as you go, wondering the whole time how he came back to "life."

That's when Zod arrives and joins the fray.

➜ **If you decide to focus on Zod, go to 14.**

➜ **If you decide to focus on Brainiac, go to 46.**

5

Must stop Zod and deal with the Peace Conference and Perry later!

"You will not defeat me so easily if you are concerned with protecting millions of your precious humans," Zod says.

Obviously he figured out how to get out of all those layers of rock.

Zod takes to the skies, flying swiftly to Metropolis. You follow and within seconds you both hover above the city.

"More difficult, eh, Kal-El?" Zod says, knowing that now you will not only have to fight him, but also worry about the safety of the city's millions of citizens. "As I said before, your feelings for these humans will be your undoing, while I have no such handicap."

Zod zooms right toward a towering skyscraper where hundreds of people are working. The street below the skyscraper is packed with pedestrians.

→ If you decide to slam into Zod and try to fly him away from the city, go to 44.

→ If you decide to send a blast of super-breath his way to knock him off course, go to 24.

6

You hover in the sky directly above the LexCorp building. *I need to stop this right now so I can get back to the Peace Conference.*

Without hesitation, you burst into the lab at LexCorp. Technicians there open a huge vault with a thick lead door. Behind the door is a large stash of Kryptonite.

You crumble to the floor of the lab. You are helpless. Everything goes dark.

THE END

7

Zod poses a huge threat to the entire human race, you think. *He has all the same powers that I do and he wants to use them to dominate the human race. I have to stop him before I do anything else. Perry and Lex will just have to wait.*

You zoom to the Rockies where you find Zod about to devastate an entire town with a blast of super-breath. Gale force winds emanate from Zod's mouth. You fly right into their path and use a blast of your own super-breath to redirect them harmlessly into the sky.

"Your attempts to stop me will prove futile, Kal-El," Zod boasts. "You cannot win this battle. Your sympathy and compassion for these pathetic humans will be the weakness that leads to your undoing."

"Quite the opposite, Zod," you shout back. "It is my compassion for all living beings that is my greatest strength—something you will never understand."

"How touching, Kal-El," Zod says mockingly. "You almost make me want to cry. But I've got other things to do with my eyes!"

Zod turns toward a nearby forest and shoots a blast of searing heat vision at a dense growth. A grove of trees bursts into flame. You instantly realize that the ensuing fire would spread and destroy the forest and the many small villages that surround it.

I've got to put out that fire!

You speed to a nearby lake. Spinning at super-speed, you draw up water from the lake all around you, then direct it toward the flames. The huge torrent of water splashes down, putting out the fire.

Just as you are relieved that you have prevented a gigantic catastrophe, Zod slams into you, driving you into a mountain. You push back, breaking your way out, but Zod still clings to you tightly.

This could go on forever, you realize. *Our powers are evenly matched. I've got to put Zod out of commission while I figure out how to get him back to the Phantom Zone.*

You grab Zod and drive him deep underground, embedding him in solid rock. For a moment he doesn't budge. *Perhaps since he is new at using superpowers he is not recovering from the blows as quickly as I did.*

Your mind once again shifts to the Peace Conference. Perry is not a patient man. You know he's going to want an update any minute, but you've been so busy battling your foes that you haven't had a moment to check in on the Peace Conference.

➔ If you decide to return to the Peace Conference, go to 22.

➔ If you decide to try to finish off Zod and send him back to the Phantom Zone, go to 5.

8

You believe that this must be some kind of prank. After all, how can Superman be elsewhere? Besides, some of your enemies have tried to make it look as if you have turned evil in the past.

You decide to keep an eye on this new situation, but you know you must return to the Peace Conference before you fall so far behind in covering the event that you'll have no chance to write the story.

You return to the conference, but it turns out that the Superman imposter is none other than General Zod, your old enemy from Krypton. Being from Krypton he has all of your powers, but having not been raised here on Earth by loving parents like Jonathon and Martha Kent as you were, he has chosen to use his great powers to conquer the world.

Your hesitation has given General Zod enough time to seize control of the Earth.

THE END

9

Multiple sites with the same alien technology all around the world cannot be a coincidence, you think as you speed through the air. Using your super-hearing as a guide, you follow one of the signals to South America.

Focusing your super-hearing to pinpoint the location of the signal, you land in a barren mountainous region. *Hmm… I'm still picking up the signal, only now it's directly under my feet.*

Peering into the rock formation, your X-ray vision penetrates the upper layers of stone, but soon runs into a deposit of lead. This blocks your X-ray vision.

Guess I have to make a personal appearance to finish my investigation.

Spinning like a drill, you bore into the solid rock, flying straight down. You plunge deeper and deeper into the Earth, passing through layer after layer. The deeper you go, the louder the signal gets.

In a few seconds you burst through the roof of a huge underground cavern, only to discover that it contains an enormous lab. In the center of the lab sits a gigantic machine with tubes and pipes snaking out in every direction.

Startled technicians in white lab coats scatter in shock at the sight of you ... all except one.

Upon spotting you, one technician hurries to the machine. He opens a lead door at the heart of the enormously complex machine, revealing a huge chunk of Kryptonite!

Should you stay in the lab or flee?

→ If you decide to try to escape from the lab, go to 60.

→ If you decide to stay, go to 59.

10

In Perry White's office, you, as Clark Kent, and Perry look at the front page of the *Daily Planet*, which carries the story you wrote about the Peace Conference.

Because of the choices you made when you battled your enemies as Superman and covered the Peace Conference as Clark Kent, you have saved the world from danger, defeated all your enemies, and managed to write the story Perry wanted to see. You have won, and Earth is safe once again. Not to mention the fact that you're on Perry's good side—at least for today!

"Well, Kent, nice job," Perry says, smiling, as he scans the *Daily Planet*'s front page. "You see, that's what happens when you stay focused on your task and don't let anything else distract you."

"I couldn't agree more, Mr. White," you reply. "I couldn't agree more."

THE END

11

You quickly fly up to the Peace Conference and hover in space right outside the orbiting space station. Using your X-ray vision to peer into the space station, you see that the delegates are all attending various meetings.

You quickly check to see that all the meetings are being recorded by the equipment you left behind.

I hate to do it, but I'm going to have to piece my article together from these recordings, while making it seem as if I actually attended each meeting!

Satisfied that you'll be able to get the stories you need later, you zoom back to Earth to finish your battle with Zod.

➜ If you decide to try to lure Zod into a trap, go to 39.

➜ If you decide to use one of your superpowers to surprise Zod, go to 12.

12

Making sure you remain far enough away so that you are not affected, you exhale a blast of super-breath that blows away the pile of debris that you had previously used to cover the Kryptonite. Zod falls to the ground, weakened by the effects of the Kryptonite.

You feel a little dizzy and step back a few feet. The dizziness passes.

"Kal-El! What have you done," Zod cries weakly. "Would you knowingly and intentionally kill me? I need your help."

Then Zod passes out.

Should I grab Zod and try to figure out what his master plan was? It might help me in the future. Or should I bring him back to my Fortress of Solitude and send him back to the Phantom Zone?

HIDDEN MESSAGE

Find the message hidden in this sentence:

MEMO FOR
SOLDIERS AT THE FORT
RE: S. S. PAYMENT

➔ If you decide to go to your Fortress of Solitude, go to 17.

➔ If you decide to grab Zod, go to 45.

13

You fly up into space and find the main LexCorp satellite that is controlling the Kryptonite web. One by one you see bright green strands of Kryptonite energy forming a web all around Earth below.

If the web is completed, I'll never be able to return to Earth! I've got to stop that satellite now!

What can you do to stop it?

→ If you decide to go to the dead Brainiac satellite, go to 54.

→ If you decide to head to the LexCorp satellite, go to 29.

MAZE

Navigate the maze to figure out which satellite to go to.

14

You turn your attention to Zod, but you realize that the two of you could battle to a stalemate forever. Then you think of the one thing you know that will stop Zod for certain.

A plan forms in your head. It's dangerous, but it is the only way you can think of to stop Zod for good.

But can you execute the plan before Brainiac gains control of the entire planet?

WORD SEARCH

Find and circle all the following words in a WORD SEARCH. Then list the remaining letters (those not circled) to reveal a clue.

GREEN   HOME   NIGHT   ROCK

G	R	E	E	N
H	O	M	E	I
K	C	R	Y	G
P	K	T	O	H
N	I	T	E	T

→ If you decide to battle Brainiac, go to 46.

→ If you think you have found a way to stop Zod, go to 3.

15

It doesn't seem as if there is an immediate threat. I think I need to stay here at the conference.

The conference continues. You do several interviews and take notes during a few panel discussions. A short while later, during a presentation, you begin to feel weak. You immediately recognize the symptoms—Kryptonite radiation!

Who could have brought Kryptonite aboard the space station? And why?

Hoping to escape the effects of the Kryptonite, you slip from the conference room, use all your remaining strength to change into Superman and fly from the space station.

But being out in space doesn't change a thing. A sickly green glow radiates from the Earth's surface, extending up into space. You grow weaker as you feel the radiation penetrate your skin.

Using your telescopic vision, you discover that Lex Luthor has set up a worldwide Kryptonite web and is bombarding Earth and space around it with powerful Kryptonite radiation. You are overcome by the Kryptonite.

THE END

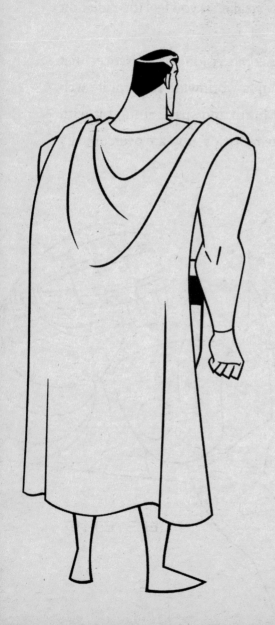

16

"This ends here, Luthor,"
you say through clenched
teeth.

Luthor remains perfectly
still, looking up from his
desk, smiling at you.

You streak across the
room ready to grab Luthor,
but even though you are trav-
eling at super-speed, Luthor
vanishes before you reach him.

Reaching the desk, you see that
he wasn't really there. Instead, a small
holographic projector sitting under
his desk was producing a holographic
image of Luthor that you triggered
by stepping into the room.

I should have realized that Luthor would not be caught that easily. And every instinct tells me that this is a trap!

Solve this puzzle to help you decide what to do next.

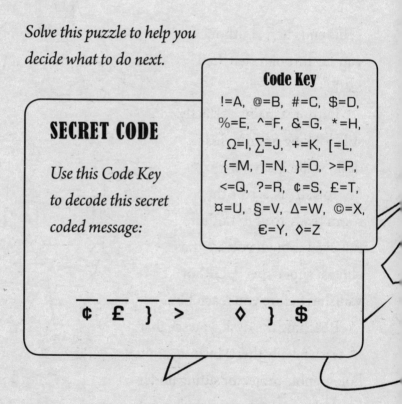

SECRET CODE

Use this Code Key to decode this secret coded message:

Code Key

!=A, @=B, #=C, $=D, %=E, ^=F, &=G, *=H, Ω=I, ∑=J, +=K, [=L, {=M,]=N, }=O, >=P, <=Q, ?=R, ¢=S, £=T, ¤=U, §=V, Δ=W, ©=X, €=Y, ◊=Z

¢ £ } >　　◊ } $

→ **If you decide to stay at LexCorp, go to 38.**

→ **If you decide to go stop Zod, go to 7.**

17

With Zod in a weakened state, you realize that this is the best chance you'll have to send him back to the Phantom Zone. You speed to your Fortress of Solitude. There you grab the Phantom Zone Projector, the gateway between Earth and the shadowy plane of existence known as the Phantom Zone, and speed back to South America.

"Time to go back where you belong, Zod!" you shout, making sure to keep your distance from the Kryptonite. You turn on the Phantom Zone Projector. Its brilliant beam surrounds the helpless Zod.

"I vow revenge, Kal-El, on you and the humans you protect!" Zod screams as he fades from view, banished once again to the nether realm of the Phantom Zone.

Another blast of your super-breath against the debris covers up the Kryptonite so you can move safely around the lab.

Two enemies down...but your most dangerous foe still remains at large and still has a plan that could destroy you forever!

➜ If you decide to go after Lex Luthor, go to 52.

➜ If you decide to go back to the Peace Conference, go to 18.

18

You return to the Peace Conference on the orbiting space station as Clark Kent, but this gives Lex Luthor enough time to complete and activate his world-wide Kryptonite web, preventing you from returning to Earth.

THE END

19

You speed back to the Peace Conference and change back to Clark Kent. The Peace Conference is wrapping up. The delegates and world leaders are preparing to head back to Earth, which is now safe again thanks to your efforts as Superman.

Well, I've succeeded at missing the entire conference thanks to the enemies of Superman. Perry will be demanding a story any second. Those videos are my only hope now.

You grab your video equipment and find a quiet room. There you review the videos of every meeting that has taken place during the entire conference, watching all of the meetings at the same time.

Your Kryptonian mind allows you to absorb every detail as if you had actually attended each meeting.

Then, typing at super-speed, you write up the story of the conference, completing it just as the space

station's security guards
ask the last few people
on the station
to leave.

➔ Go to 10.

20

I'll have to deal with Perry's impatience later, you think. *Zod is just too dangerous!*

Remembering the Kryptonite buried beneath the rubble in the underground LexCorp lab in South America, you fly there, knowing that Zod will follow you.

Which is exactly what he does.

"Why have you come to this place?" Zod demands.

"I've decided that I can't defeat you," you say to Zod.

He eyes you curiously, knowing you well enough to realize that this is a ploy of some kind.

"What trick are you planning, Kal-El?" Zod says cautiously. "I know you, and you would never simply give up."

You've got him right where you want him.

Suddenly, the image of Perry White pacing back and forth in his office, muttering about Clark Kent and his coverage of the Peace Conference, pops into your mind. You start to get anxious about keeping up with your assignment as Clark Kent. But one of your greatest foes is right in front of you.

What do you do next?

→ If you decide to return to the Peace Conference, go to 11.

→ If you decide to retreat to the far side of the lab, go to 39.

21

The alien origin of the signal troubles you. Also, this talk of a web around the world smacks of something very wrong.

You decide to take to the air. Lifting off from the roof of the LexCorp building, you zoom into space. Once out in space, you fly around the Earth several times, scanning the globe with your telescopic vision, searching for similar technology.

To your shock, you discover about a dozen places scattered around the globe that all have the same type of technological signature. And they are all projecting a guidance signal that breaks through the Earth's atmosphere and reaches up many miles above the planet.

This is a huge, worldwide system. I have got to investigate further.

➔ If you decide to stop at a few of the places for a closer look, go to 9.

➔ If you decide to return to LexCorp in Metropolis, go to 26.

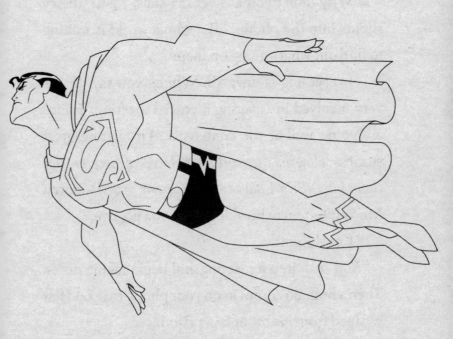

22

You fly back to the space station and change to Clark Kent. You look at your phone and see several missed calls—all from Perry White. You call him.

"Why didn't you answer my calls, Kent?" Perry shouts into the phone. "The whole world is waiting to find out what's going on there!"

"Everything is fine, Mr. White," you say. "I was very involved in covering a crucial meeting. Things are going well at the conference. I'm getting great stories." *How in the world will I ever deliver on this claim later when I have to write up my article?* "Sorry, Mr. White, you're breaking up. Gotta go. Bye."

"Kent! Kent!"

You rush into a meeting and begin taking notes. Then a bulletin comes in on your phone that Zod has escaped from his mountain prison.

If I don't get some time here to cover the conference I may have to find a new job as Clark Kent. Then again if I don't stop Zod the point may be moot!

Do you stay or go?

SOLVE THE PUZZLE ON THE NEXT PAGE TO FIGURE OUT YOUR NEXT MOVE.

UNSCRAMBLE

Unscramble the following words and write them in the spaces. Then read down the circled column to get a clue as to what you should do.

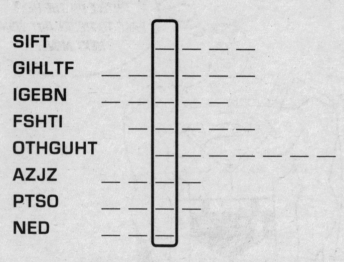

SIFT

GIHLTF

IGEBN

FSHTI

OTHGUHT

AZJZ

PTSO

NED

→ If you decide to stay at the conference, go to 36.

→ If you decide to go back to battle Zod, go to 5.

23

Landing on the roof of the LexCorp building, you use your X-ray vision to scan the interior. Peering down through all the floors of the enormous skyscraper, you look into a vast underground workshop where a huge high-tech device is being assembled by a team of technicians.

Luthor is working on something big, you think. *That's not unusual. Still, some of the radiation frequencies I've been picking up are not earthly in origin, and that's what concerns me.*

You train your super-hearing on the workshop.

"Where are we?" asks a muffled voice.

"We are moments away from connecting the rest of the web around the world," replies another voice.

"Good," says the first voice. "I want no more delays."

"Yes, sir!" says the frightened second voice.

Hard to tell what they are doing. And what kind of web are they talking about? A web around the world? What kind of web could that be?

→ If you decide to return to the conference, go to 15.

→ If you decide to search for other similar technology, go to 21.

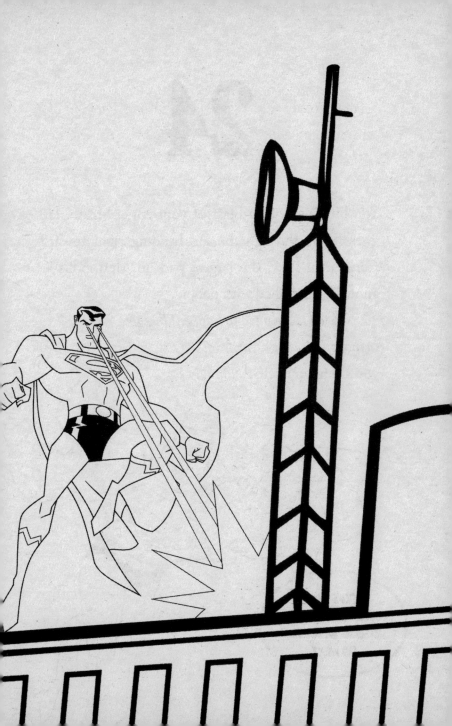

24

You hit Zod with a blast of your super-breath. He goes flying through the air, heading right toward Centennial Park, the largest park in Metropolis— another place filled with people.

Not what I wanted to happen! I've got to move the battle away from the city, you say to yourself. *But how?*

SOLVE THIS PUZZLE TO HELP YOU DECIDE WHAT TO DO NEXT.

HIDDEN MESSAGE

Find the hidden message in this sentence:

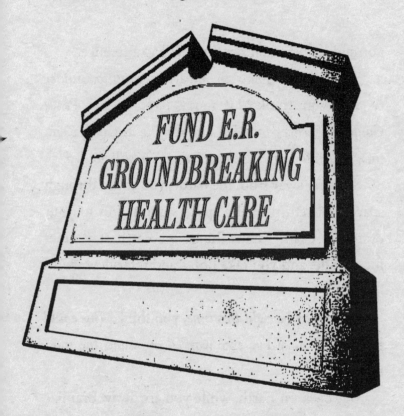

FUND E.R. GROUNDBREAKING HEALTH CARE

→ If you decide to fly Zod into space, go to 57.

→ If you decide to slam Zod to the ground, go to 51.

25

You suddenly remember the Peace Conference.

The military seems to have this situation under control, you think. *I'll hurry back to the Peace Conference, check on what's happening as Clark Kent, then return to Earth as Superman if I'm still needed.*

Slipping away from the battle, you zoom through space and return to the space station, and to your duties as Clark Kent. Things on Earth stay quiet for a while, and you take notes and interview world leaders.

Perry may be right this time, you think. *This could be the best story I've ever worked on—and the most important.*

But back on Earth, while you are away, Brainiac 2.5 sends many more copies of his android self to Earth. Brainiac infiltrates the world's computer systems so quickly there is nothing anyone can do to stop him.

It is too late. Brainiac 2.5 has seized control of the world.

THE END

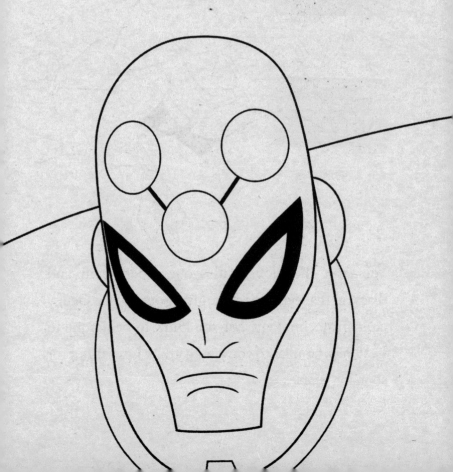

26

You scan the globe with your super-vision and discover that every machine giving out this frequency contains technology that you know to be unique to LexCorp, familiar to you after battling Lex Luthor for so many years.

This all comes back to Lex, you realize. *Which means it's got to end with him as well.*

You zoom back to Metropolis.

➜ If you decide to burst into the lab at LexCorp, go to 6.

➜ If you find yourself distracted by another incident, go to 40.

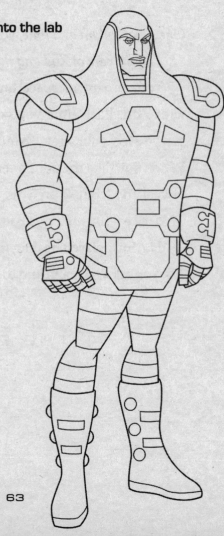

27

One super-villain at a time, you think.

I'll take care of Zod and then deal with Brainiac.

You remain in space and continue your battle with Zod. Each time you come near Earth's yellow sun you feel your strength increase. But so does Zod's. When you take the fight out of this solar system, Zod is weakened, but so are you.

This evenly matched battle goes on and on.

Having delayed dealing with the threat of Brainiac 2.5, you allow the android to gain control of Earth.

THE END

28

Hmm, you think, pondering the appearance of the additional androids around the world. *These androids have so far posed no threat, and I'm scheduled to cover the opening meeting. I think I'll stay on the space station and monitor the situation from here.*

The Peace Conference begins. One by one, world leaders step up to the podium and give their opening remarks. You're surprised that you have gotten no further updates from Jimmy, but you feel like you can stay put for now.

You jot down notes as the opening to your article begins to take shape in your mind.

Nothing from Jimmy, you think as the meeting progresses. *I guess these androids may not be the threat I thought they would be.*

But what you don't realize is that the androids have cut off all communication between Earth and the space station. That's why you still haven't heard from Jimmy.

In the end, these androids turn out to be bodies created by Brainiac 2.5, each of which contains his computer-like mind. He infiltrates the main computer networks of governments, corporations, and militaries worldwide. He renders planet Earth inoperative.

While all the world leaders are away at the Peace Conference, Brainiac 2.5 easily gains control of the entire world.

THE END

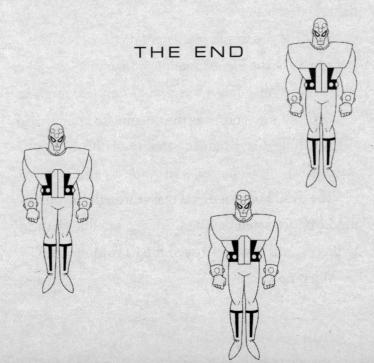

29

You try to approach the LexCorp satellite but start to feel weak from the effects of the Kryptonite surging through it.

That's not going to work, you think. *I can't even get near the thing.*

That's when you spot the dead Brainiac satellite floating in space.

That's it! you think. *Just what I need!*

You fly to the lifeless satellite and grab it.

I'm only going to get one shot at this. Got to make it count.

You fling the Brainiac satellite at the LexCorp satellite.

The dead hunk of metal tears through the pulsating LexCorp satellite. The LexCorp satellite shatters to pieces. You have destroyed the Kryptonite web.

What now?

HIDDEN MESSAGE

To help figure out your next move, find the hidden message in this sentence:

➜ **Go to 19.**

30

You speed after Brainiac, knowing that he must be stopped.

I'd love to know what he's up to, you think, *but first I've got to disarm him!*

Slamming into Brainiac at super-speed, you shift the course of his flight, sending his metallic body crashing right into his own Omega Spears.

I may have been able to use Brainiac's own weapons against him.

But much to your surprise, the Omega Spears are absorbed back into Brainiac's body. They don't harm him, but at least you have stopped the Omega Spears from shooting into the Washington Monument.

I should have guessed, you think. *Since Brainiac created the weapons based on his own internal circuitry, they would not hurt him.*

Now it's Brainiac's turn. He flies at you, slamming into your body, driving you into the ground. His robotic strength is almost a match for your Kryptonian abilities.

You manage to free yourself from his grasp, but realize that you have other problems to deal with as well.

This battle is far from over, but you still need to battle with the other Brainiac 2.5, the one that is attacking government offices in Paris, not to mention your responsibilities as Clark Kent at the Peace Conference.

→ If you think you should stay and battle this Brainiac 2.5, go to 49.

→ If you think you should focus on the Brainiac 2.5 in Paris, go to 31.

31

Knowing that the threat of Brainiac 2.5 is spreading, you hurry to Paris.

Even though I can fly at super-speed, I can't be in ten places at once, you think. *I'll have to neutralize this threat one Brainiac at a time.*

In Paris, you find the French military engaged in a fierce battle with the android. The army blasts Brainiac with artillery fire, but he deflects the blows, redirecting the weapons so that they explode into the ground.

The battle rages back and forth. Additional French troops arrive, but Brainiac escalates his attacks to greet them.

Then Brainiac unleashes a barrage of Omega Spears right at the French military commander. You fly at super-speed and place yourself between the two adversaries. Bracing yourself for the impact, you deflect the Omega Spears harmlessly away.

I've got to take more direct action, you say to yourself. *Can't keep playing defense all the time with the threat happening all over the world! I've got to do something right now!*

But what should your next move be?

→ If you decide to use Brainiac's computer-like brain against him, go to 48.

→ If you unleash a straight-on attack, go to 58.

32

You realize that you've got to go cover the Peace Conference. This time, Perry would not accept any excuses. Your career as Clark Kent, so essential to your work as Superman, depends on getting this story of major significance.

But you'll certainly keep an eye on the android story as well.

"Thanks, Jimmy," you say. "I've got to leave for the Peace Conference. But please keep me posted on the android."

"Sure thing, Mr. Kent," Jimmy says. "I'll shoot you off a text if anything new comes across."

You board a chartered space shuttle that soon blasts off, taking you and the other reporters to the space station. As Earth recedes out the shuttle's window, you think again of how important your adopted planet Earth is to you. You have sworn to protect and defend Earth using your powers as Superman. But right now, you need to focus on getting this story. When you arrive at the space station, you see delegates from every country in the world gathering for the historic event.

Let's see, you say to yourself, looking over the list of interviews you have to do and the number of events and meetings you have to cover. *Phew, I'm going to be busy from the minute I wake up to the minute I go to sleep every day for the next week. This time Perry may be right. This could be the assignment of a lifetime. Still, I'll need to stay alert for any updates on the android from Jimmy.*

As you are organizing your schedule, word comes in that additional, identical androids have suddenly appeared in Europe, Russia, and China, all demanding to see the government leaders.

WORD SEARCH

Find and circle all the following words in a word search.
Then list the remaining letters (those not circled) to
reveal a clue.

CLARK   ROBOT   ORBIT   MEETS

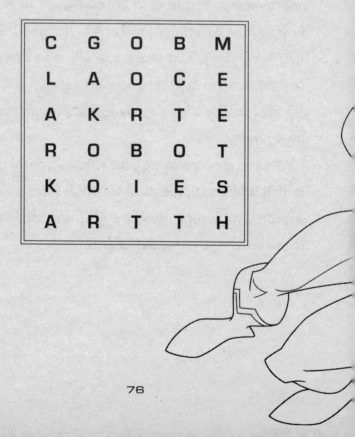

C	G	O	B	M
L	A	O	C	E
A	K	R	T	E
R	O	B	O	T
K	O	I	E	S
A	R	T	T	H

➜ After solving the puzzle, if you think you should stay at the conference, go to 28.

➜ If you think you should sneak away, change into Superman, and go to Earth to investigate, go to 53.

33

Fearing for the safety of the residents of Metropolis, and of Earth in general, you decide to take the battle to the moon.

Grabbing Zod tightly, you fly up through Earth's atmosphere and out into space. Reaching the moon, you hurry to the dark side.

Suddenly you feel Zod weaken in your grip.

The lack of direct yellow sun must be weakening him, you realize.

But of course, it also weakens you.

You and Zod crash to the moon's surface.

You shove Zod away with a blast of super-breath, sending him tumbling through the fine gray dust.

Zod whacks you with a double-fisted punch that sends you reeling and tumbling in the fine gray powder.

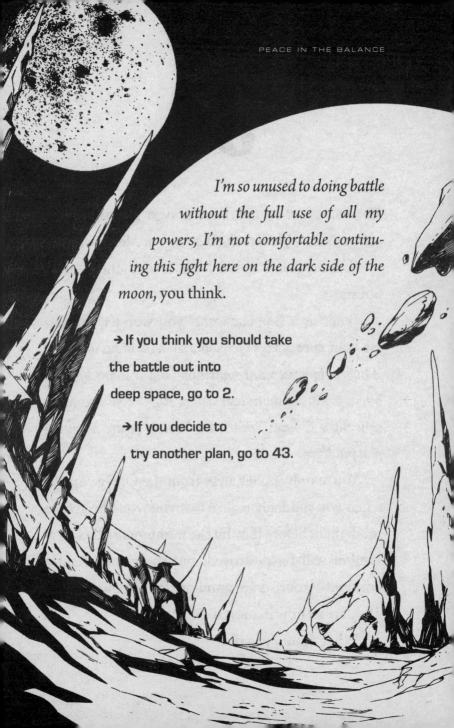

I'm so unused to doing battle without the full use of all my powers, I'm not comfortable continuing this fight here on the dark side of the moon, you think.

→ **If you think you should take the battle out into deep space, go to 2.**

→ **If you decide to try another plan, go to 43.**

34

No choice. Got to stop those Omega Spears! They're going to slam right into the Washington Monument!

You turn and speed back toward the Omega Spears.

What does Brainiac want? you wonder, increasing your speed. *He's incredibly smart and his database is huge. He must want something, but it seems he's just interested in random destruction. Right now I've got to stop those Omega Spears. I'll have to figure Brainac's plot out later.*

You're only inches away from the Omega Spears when you suddenly realize that you won't be able to reach them before they hit the monument. This great symbol will be destroyed, but more importantly, hundred of tourists are standing near the monument. They are all now in mortal danger!

What should you do?

UNSCRAMBLE

Unscramble the following words and write them in the spaces. Then read down the circled column.

SOLVE THIS PUZZLE TO HELP YOU DECIDE WHAT TO DO NEXT.

AECHS __ __ __ __ __

ETEDAF __ __ __ __ __ __

YRA __ __ __

TKACAT __ __ __ __ __ __

VASE __ __ __ __

SKIR __ __ __ __

POTS __ __ __ __

HIFTG __ __ __ __ __

RSRDOE __ __ __ __ __ __

ABINR __ __ __ __ __

➜ If you decide to use Brainiac himself to stop the Omega Spears, go to 30.

➜ If you decide to use one of your own powers, go to 49.

35

I need to stop Brainiac once and for all before I can turn my attention to finishing off Zod.

You zoom off into space. Using your super-hearing to track the signals beaming to Brainiac, you locate the satellite that houses his consciousness.

Unless I'm mistaken, all that remains of Brainiac 2.5 is contained in the circuits of this satellite.

You fire an intense beam of heat vision at the satellite, destroying its circuitry. Then for good measure you rip out the satellite's main processing unit and hurl it into the sun, where it immediately burns up.

You return to Earth and find the Brainiac android a lifeless heap.

One threat stopped, you sign in relief. *But where is Zod?*

Zod is nowhere in sight.

I'm not sure where to even start looking for Zod, you think. *Still, he must be stopped. But at the moment, all I can think about is Perry's blood pressure going up as he wonders why he hasn't gotten an update from me in a while. Maybe I should go back to the Peace Conference so I can report in to Perry.*

→ If you decide to go after Zod, go to 20.

→ If you decide to return to the Peace Conference as Clark Kent so you can report back to Perry, go to 11.

36

You decide to stay at the Peace Conference, get one more story to satisfy Perry, and then go deal with Zod.

But while you're at the space station, Zod uses his superpowers to go on a rampage. One by one he gains control of country after country. No militaries or weapons on Earth can stop him. He quickly conquers the world.

THE END

37

You quickly fly over to the general in charge.

"General, what's going on here?" you ask. "Why have you opened fire?"

"I was making a pre-emptive strike, Superman," the general explains.

"General, I have had dealings with this android before," you explain. "If you would order a halt to the artillery barrage, maybe I can find out what he wants."

"Very well, Superman," the general agrees. Then he signals his troops to stop firing at Brainiac 2.5.

Where a moment before the air was filled with the deafening roar of gunfire, now a tension-filled silence descends. Brainiac stands perfectly still, like a statue. Slowly you walk toward your longtime adversary.

"Brainiac," you call out. "What are you doing here? What is it you want this time?"

No reply. Brainiac remains still.

You move closer.

"I have gotten the army to stop firing at you," you point out. "I have shown you my good faith. Now tell me what you want."

You catch a tiny glint of light in Brainiac's eyes a split second before he raises his arms and fires two Omega Spears right at you, at point-blank range.

The powerful weapons streak through the air.

Catching you off guard, the spears slam into your chest, knocking you backward. You tumble to the ground, unhurt yet startled by the abruptness of the attack.

As you climb to your feet, the general rushes to your side. "Superman, we've just received word that another android is attacking government offices in Paris," he says.

→ If you decide to attack Brainiac here in Washington, go to **47**.

→ If you decide to fly to Paris, leaving the army to take care of this situation, go to **31**.

38

"Tricked by Luthor!" you exclaim. "He's not here. He's probably not even in the building."

At that moment your super-hearing picks up a report of more destruction by Zod. And, as if you needed something else to deal with, as you prepare to investigate Zod, as you prepare to investigate, you begin to grow concerned about covering the Peace Conference as Clark Kent.

It's only a matter of time before Perry wants to know what's going on at the Peace Conference. I really should know what's happening there. So what do I do? Do I go after Zod or do I go back o the Peace Conference as Clark Kent?

Finding Lex and stopping his Kryptonite machine will have to wait.

→ If you decide to go after Zod, go to 7.

→ If you decide to return to the Peace Conference, go to 22.

39

You move across the underground lab to get as far away from Zod as you can get.

"Are you truly frightened of me, Kal-El?" Zod asks, sounding genuinely surprised. "The son of Jor-El has proven himself to be as much of a coward as his father was."

That's it, Zod, keep running your mouth. It's what you're good at after all.

Now it's time to make your move.

SOLVE THE PUZZLE ON THE NEXT PAGE TO HELP YOU CHOOSE WHICH SUPERPOWER TO USE.

UNSCRAMBLE

Unscramble the following words and write them in the spaces. Then read down the circled column to get a clue about where you should go next.

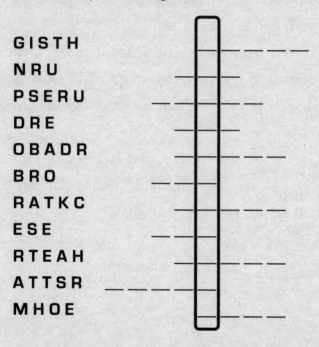

GISTH

NRU

PSERU

DRE

OBADR

BRO

RATKC

ESE

RTEAH

ATTSR

MHOE

→ If you decide to use your super-breath, go to 12.

→ If you decide to attack Zod with your super-strength, go to 45.

40

You decide to investigate the strange report of Superman destroying the world. This is not the first time one of your enemies has tried to make it look as if you have turned evil.

You track the destruction all across the country, finally ending up in the Rocky Mountains. There you see what appears to be a man flying into a mountain, smashing it to bits.

Okay, you think. *Who besides me can do something like that?*

The terrible answer becomes horribly clear.

Zooming overhead, you discover that the man is General Zod, a Kryptonian villain who has escaped from the Phantom Zone. The Phantom Zone is an alternate dimension discovered by your Kryptonian father, Jor-El.

It is used as a place to send criminals to keep them isolated. General Zod tried to gain control of Krypton. Jor-el banished him to the Phantom Zone. And now…he has returned to take out his revenge on you!

And to make matters worse, here on Earth, under its yellow sun, Zod has the same powers as you do.

"Zod, this ends now!" you shout.

"Kal-El, once again you prove yourself a fool for using your superior powers to help the pathetic, weak people of Earth," Zod answers, using your Kryptonian name. "You should be ruling this clearly inferior race. But it doesn't matter—after I dispose of you, I will subject the people of Earth to my complete domination!"

"I won't allow that, Zod!" you shout back.

Should you battle Zod right now or go back to LexCorp to stop Lex Luthor's Kryptonite machine?

MAZE

Make your way through this maze to decide where you go next.

→ If you choose to go to LexCorp, go to 50.

→ If you choose to battle Zod, go to 7.

41

Because of your superpowers like super-hearing, you are always becoming aware of unusual activities around the world.

I really need to cover the Peace Conference, you think. *If a dangerous situation on Earth presents itself, I won't be far away up on the space station. And I really need to get this story.*

You fly back up to the space station and quickly change into Clark Kent just in time for an important meeting. As you take notes your cell phone vibrates. Slipping quietly from the conference room, you answer it. It's Perry White.

"Kent, how's it going?" Perry asks.

"Fine, Mr. White," you reply. "As a matter of fact, you pulled me out of a meeting."

"Well, get back in there, Kent!" Perry bellows. "What do you think you're doing?!"

"Yes, sir," you reply. Then you hang up and head back into the conference.

A few minutes later, your super-hearing picks up more strange technological activity in Metropolis.

This sounds odd, but not necessarily dangerous, you think.

➜ If you stay at the conference, go to 15.

➜ If you go to Metropolis, go to 56.

42

You rush at Luthor and grab him.

"Turn the weapon off, Luthor!" you demand.

"Or what, Superman?" Luthor cackles. "You'll kill me? You know you won't do that. You have no option here...but to die a horrible death from Kryptonite radiation."

As angry as you are, you know that Lex Luthor is absolutely right. You will never take a life, regardless of how evil the person whose life it is may be.

I'm not going to get any help from Luthor, you realize, releasing him. *I'm going to have to stop this Kryptonite web myself.*

But how?

➜ If you decide to fly to the LexCorp satellite, go to 13.

➜ If you have another plan in mind, go to 54.

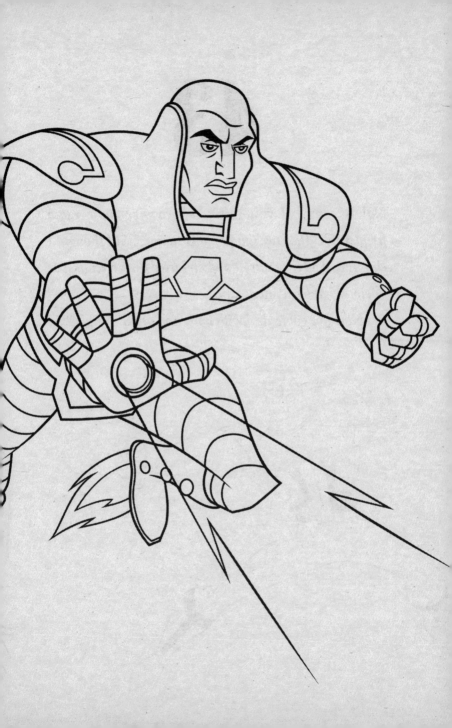

43

No! It can't be! you think. I recognize those radio frequencies. They are unique to Brainiac 2.5! I thought I eliminated all the androids when I fried their circuits, but obviously at least one escaped.

Now I've got to deal with both Zod and Brainiac 2.5!

→ If you decide to continue your battle with Zod, go to 27.

→ If you decide to fly back to Earth, go to 4.

44

No time to waste. Too many people, you think, speeding toward Zod.

"We're taking this fight as far away from Metropolis as possible!" you shout.

You fly right at Zod, grab him around the waist and direct him away from the building.

"I suggest we stay right here!" Zod snaps back at you.

He matches your strength and starts to drive you down toward the street.

"Two can play this game, Kal-El," Zod insists. "As I said, we are staying right here!"

→ If you decide to use another of your powers to battle Zod, go to 24.

→ If you decide to try to slam Zod to the ground, go to 51.

45

You fly right at Zod to use your super-strength, but in the ensuing struggle you are exposed to the Kryptonite. As a result both of you are left powerless.

THE END

46

I must stop Brainiac 2.5 once and for all.

You continue your battle with Brainiac.

As you deflect his Omega Spears and he avoids your blasts of heat vision, your super-hearing detects radio signals being downloaded from space...right to Brainiac 2.5!

That's it! That's how he survived. He must have uploaded his programming to an orbiting satellite just before I destroyed his android bodies. That way he was able to reconstruct himself and continue his attack on Earth.

I've got to destroy that satellite and eliminate the threat of Brainiac once and for all.

"Did you forget about me, Kal-El?" Zod shouts. "These distractions will not spare you defeat at my hands!"

I can't be in two places at once! I need to decide who to battle first.

→ If you decide to try to stop Zod, go to 3.

→ If you decide to destroy the satellite, go to 35 .

47

No time for diplomacy, you think. *I've dealt with Brainiac before and he is after only one thing—the destruction of the entire planet!*

You fly directly at Brainiac, fists clenched, determined to stop him.

Brainiac fires his Omega Spears at you. You shift your flight path slightly to avoid the attack. The streaking Omega Spears zip harmlessly past you.

But glancing back over your shoulder, you see that the Omega Spears are now headed right for the Washington Monument.

Stopping Brainiac will have to wait. I've got to stop those spears from hitting the Washington Monument.

At that moment, Brainiac charges right at the army troops.

→ If you decide to try to stop the Omega Spears, go to 34.

→ If you go after Brainiac to protect the army troops, go to 30.

48

Suddenly, the French commander announces that a report has just come in that Brainiac androids are attacking in London, Madrid, Beijing, and Tokyo, all at the same time!

Battling android after android around the world will take too much time. I won't be able to stop them all! you realize.

Then you spot an overhead power line. The line has been severed and is sizzling and sparking from damage it sustained during the battle.

Someone could get hurt, you think. *Which gives me an idea! If all goes well I'll be able to neutralize the threat of all the Brainiac androids once and for all!*

You swiftly fly up to the power line, which is writhing wildly through the air like an electric snake. Grabbing the sparking wire, you fly directly at Brainiac.

Have to time this just right.

You fire a blast of heat vision right at Brainiac's head. He lifts his arms to deflect the blow, which is exactly what you had hoped he would do.

As Brainiac raises his arms, he leaves the opening in his chest armor fully exposed.

Reaching the android, you shove the live, high-voltage wire right into the chest opening of Brainiac's armor.

High-voltage energy surges into Brainiac, frying his computer circuits—not just here in Paris, but throughout the world. The Brainiac in front of you collapses to the ground in a smoldering heap.

Your previous experience tells you that the Brainiac androids are networked. When this one fried, all of the Brainiac 2.5 consciousness in all the robots around the world suffered a complete programming meltdown. This should take care of the entire worldwide threat that the android posed.

Now to get back to that Peace Conference.

But just as the threat of Brainiac 2.5 has been neutralized and you prepare to take off for the space station, your super-hearing picks up a report of a strange technological phenomenon coming from Metropolis.

→ **If you decide to return to the Peace Conference, go to 41.**

→ **If you decide to go to Metropolis, go to 56.**

49

One Brainiac at a time, you say to yourself. *Got to stop this one first.*

Taking careful aim, you fire a blast of heat vision. The searing beams destroy the Omega Spears Brainiac had fired, then streak toward Brainiac at close to the speed of light.

But Brainiac's computer-based brain and robotic body allow him to swiftly dodge the blast.

Brainiac fires Omega Spears at you again, but you raise your arms and deflect them harmlessly into the ground.

Need a new strategy, you think.

You unleash a gust of incredibly cold super-breath, hoping to freeze up Brainiac's circuits.

Brainiac stops in place. His body begins to glow bright red as the android increases his body temperature and melts your icy blast.

You continue to use your great arsenal of powers to try to stop Brainiac. Grabbing the android's head, you twist it using your super-strength. But Brainiac's robotic body is strong and resilient. His head snaps back into place and he manages to fling you away from his body.

This battle could go on forever, you realize. *Brainiac is one enemy that can just about match my strength, speed, and strategies. Meanwhile, it appears that the army is holding its own against Brainiac. Maybe my abilities would be better used elsewhere. And this threat is bigger than simply this one android. Still, I hate to leave this job half finished!*

You debate what to do next.

Solve this puzzle to help you decide what to do next.

Code Key

!=A, @=B, #=C, $=D,
%=E, ^=F, &=G, *=H,
Ω=I, ∑=J, +=K, [=L,
{=M,]=N, }=O, >=P,
<=Q, ?=R, ¢=S, £=T,
¤=U, §=V, Δ=W, ©=X,
€=Y, ◊=Z

SECRET CODE

Use this Code Key to decode this secret coded message:

$$\underline{}\;\underline{}\quad \underline{}\;\underline{}\quad \underline{}\;\underline{}\;\underline{}\;\underline{}$$

& } £ } > ! ? Ω ¢

→ If you decide to go to Paris to confront the other android, go to 31.

→ If you decide to return to the Peace Conference as Clark Kent, go to 25.

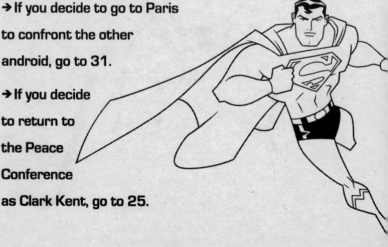

50

If I take on Zod right now, Luthor may get the time he needs to complete his Kryptonite web, you think. *If that happens, it won't matter about Zod, since that would spell the end of both of us. I must stop Luthor first, then deal with Zod later.*

"Zod, you are the fool for believing that the great powers you receive from Earth's yellow sun should be used to dominate," you shout back. "All beings deserve respect, and I use my power to see that they get it."

"Then prepare to die!" Zod bellows.

"I'll take a rain check on that, Zod," you crack. "Right now I've got to do something that will save both our lives."

You take off, streaking from the Rockies back to Metropolis in a flash. Moving at super-speed, you slip past all security at LexCorp headquarters.

You burst into Lex Luthor's office.

"Welcome, Superman. I've been expecting you," says Luthor.

→ If you rush at Luthor to force him to tell you what's going on, go to 16.

→ If you bide your time, go to 38.

51

You grasp Zod tightly, fly him to a remote corner of the city, and slam him into the ground. Driving straight down using all your tremendous strength, you bore through the sidewalk and the landfill. You keep going until you hit the solid bedrock that supports Metropolis's many huge skyscrapers.

Deeper you go, spinning and boring right through the bedrock.

You emerge into a cavern deep beneath the city's bedrock.

"At least down here, deep under the city, no innocents will be hurt," you say.

"Really?" Zod sneers. "Fool!"

Once you are in the cavern, Zod regains his footing and fights back, driving you into the solid rock wall. You feel the entire bedrock shake.

"Bringing us down here will cause greater damage!" Zod cackles. "I can destroy the entire city all at once. Thank you, Kal-El. You have saved me a great deal of time!"

This is not good. This battle is shaking the very foundation of the city. I'm endangering more lives down here than I would if we fought on the surface.

You realize that nowhere is safe from the impact of two superpowered Kryptonians doing battle... nowhere on Earth, that is.

→ If you decide to take your battle to the moon, go to 33.

→ If you decide that even the moon isn't far enough away from Earth, go to 2.

52

You hurry back to LexCorp headquarters in Metropolis. This time you find the real Lex Luthor waiting. You confront your oldest enemy.

"You're too late, Superman," Luthor says when you burst into his office. "There's nowhere for you to hide! The satellite controlling my Kryptonite web is about to be activated. Then there will be nowhere on Earth that you will be safe!"

"Seems you've gone through an awful lot of trouble just to get rid of me," you say, trying to buy some time to formulate a plan of attack.

"Don't sell yourself short, my friend," Lex says, sneering. "With you out of the way, my life immediately becomes much easier. You are worth all the effort."

Should I attack Luthor or should I head up into space?

→ If you decide to attack Luthor, go to 42.

→ If you decide to fly up into space, go to 13.

53

This smacks of the work of Brainiac 2.5,
you think. I'll have to slip away and
speed back to the conference
later. If I don't stop the threat
of Brainiac 2.5, there may not
be an Earth left to return to!

You leave the conference
room just before the opening meeting is about to start,
and find a quiet corner of
the space station. There you
quickly change into Superman.

Slipping unnoticed from the
space station's airlock, you fly to
Earth. Landing in Washington, you
find army troops stationed on the
National Mall, blasting the android.

You have a long history with Brainiac in his various forms, but this version of the android has not yet revealed his hostile intentions.

It is Brainiac 2.5, but he doesn't seem to be attacking, you say to yourself.

Artillery blasts go off all around you.

This is very strange. Why is the army firing at him? I'd like to try to find out what he wants before we blindly attack him! And the artillery fire seems to have no effect on him anyway! Still, he is one of my most dangerous enemies.

→ If you decide to ask the general in charge of the troops to stop firing so you can try to find out what Brainiac 2.5 wants, go to 37.

→ If you decide to attack Brainiac 2.5, go to 47.

Flying at super-speed, you zoom to the satellite that had controlled Brainiac.

Let's use this thing for something good! you say to yourself as you hurry back to the LexCorp satellite. Summoning all your super-strength, you hurl the huge, lifeless hunk of metal and circuits into the main

LexCorp satellite. The LexCorp satellite explodes from the impact and Lex Luthor's Kryptonite web is destroyed.

What now?

SECRET CODE

Use this Code Key to decode this secret coded message:

Code Key

!=A, @=B, #=C, $=D,
%=E, ^=F, &=G, *=H,
Ω=I, ∑=J, +=K, [=L,
{=M,]=N, }=O, >=P,
<=Q, ?=R, ¢=S, £=T,
¤=U, §=V, Δ=W, ©=X,
€=Y, ◊=Z

`> % ! # %   # } ] ^ % ? % ] # %`

➔ Go to 19.

55

You stop for a moment, wondering what to do. The conflict between your life as Clark Kent and your life as Superman is an ongoing struggle. You need your Clark Kent identity. It protects those you care about from the enemies of Superman. You simply can't risk doing a poor job covering a story like this one that has worldwide consequences.

On the other hand, you cannot shirk the solemn commitment you have made to protect and defend your adopted planet as the Man of Steel. The struggle continues, but you finally come to a decision.

You get up and start to leave Perry's office.

"And just where do you think you're going, Kent?" Perry asks.

"I want to check on this android story," you reply.

"You already have your assignment," Perry says.

"I'll be at the Peace Conference. Don't worry, Mr. White."

"I always worry, Kent!" Perry shoots back. "Comes with the territory."

"Yes, sir," you say. Then you slip from his office, followed closely by Jimmy. "Now, Jimmy, let's see what you've got on that android," you say.

Jimmy shows you a report, complete with a picture of the android in Washington D.C.

"Hmm," you say. But what you think is: *Brainiac 2.5! I've got to get to Washington. The Peace Conference will have to wait.*

You slip off and change into Superman!

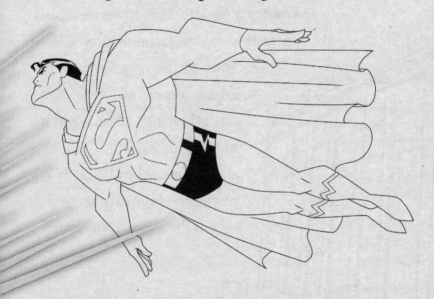

Zooming through the sky, you quickly arrive in Washington. You are right—the android is Brainiac 2.5. But as soon as he spots you, he blasts you with a Kryptonite weapon.

THE END

56

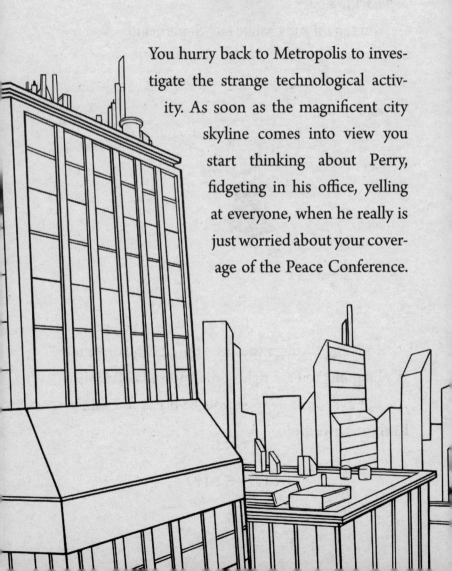

You hurry back to Metropolis to investigate the strange technological activity. As soon as the magnificent city skyline comes into view you start thinking about Perry, fidgeting in his office, yelling at everyone, when he really is just worried about your coverage of the Peace Conference.

As always, you must work on the delicate balancing act between your life as Superman and your life as Clark Kent.

You decide to zoom up to the Peace Conference quickly to see what's happening there.

You arrive at the space station and settle in at a meeting.

But while attending several events at the Peace Conference, you find it harder and harder to stay focused on the meetings. Every instinct tells you to return to Earth, to Metropolis, to investigate the strange technological activity.

Something about this technology is oddly familiar. I have to check it out.

Slipping silently from the conference room, you leave your portable video recorder running so you'll be able to catch up on important events at the conference later. Changing back to Superman, you fly to Earth.

Scanning the skies above Metropolis, your super-hearing picks up the source of the strange tech signals. You follow the signals directly to LexCorp—headquarters of your greatest enemy, Lex Luthor.

No wonder the signal was so familiar. It's LexCorp technology! Lex Luthor is up to something... again!

HIDDEN MESSAGE

Solve this puzzle to help you decide what to do next.
Find the hidden message in this sentence:

➜ If you decide to go right to LexCorp, go to 23.

➜ If you decide to see if there is any other similar technological activity in any other cities, go to 21.

57

I'm taking this battle away—very far away!

You grab Zod and fly up out of Earth's atmosphere, but the closer you get to the sun, the stronger Zod gets. Your own strength increases too, but the battle is still a stalemate.

The yellow sun of Earth is the source of both of our strength. The closer we get the stronger we get, but no one has an advantage!

Lead Superman through this maze to see where you should go next.

➔ If you decide to go to Earth, go to 51.

➔ If you decide to go to the moon, go to 33.

MAZE

Navigate the maze to either go back to Earth or go to the moon.

58

Suddenly Brainiac dashes off, flying through the streets of Paris.

Not that fast! You think.

You won't get away from me!

You take off after him.

> **FOLLOW THIS MAZE TO GET TO BRAINIAC.**

START

You reach Brainiac, but your super-hearing picks up a report of a strange technological phenomenon coming from Metropolis.

→ To use Brainiac's computer-like brain against him, go to 48.

→ To go to Metropolis, go to 56.

59

You instantly feel a massive dose of Kryptonite radiation slam into you with incredible force. You feel your powers draining quickly, knowing that once all your powers are gone, your very life force will follow.

Any attempt to fly back out of this deep cavern would be futile.

I've got to put something between me and the Kryptonite, you think.

Mustering your last remaining bit of strength, you fire a blast of your heat vision at the ceiling.

An avalanche of rocks tumbles down, burying the Kryptonite under tons of stone. The radiation is blocked and the effects of the Kryptonite begin to wear off. Slowly your strength and powers return.

As you try to figure out how all these Kryptonite machines are connected, your super-hearing picks up a news report of Superman gone crazy—flying wildly, destroying buildings, shooting his heat vision at mountaintops.

What is this now? you wonder. *Superman gone crazy?* What should you do?

TO FIGURE
OUT YOUR NEXT MOVE,
SOLVE THE PUZZLE ON
THE NEXT PAGE.

WORD SEARCH

Find and circle all the following words in a word search. Then list the remaining letters (those not circled) to reveal a clue.

AIR   FLY   XRAY   HEAT   FIT

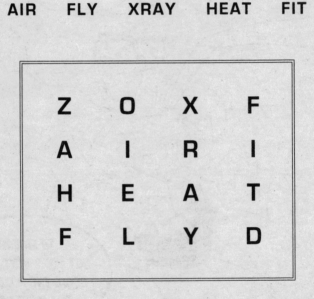

Z O X F
A I R I
H E A T
F L Y D

→ If you decide to return to the Peace Conference, go to 8.

→ If you decide to investigate, go to 40.

60

I must escape, you think, *This Kryptonite will destroy me.*

But you are growing weaker by the second. You attempt to fly back up through the narrow tunnel you created on the way down, but barely make it up to the ceiling of the cavern before you weaken and plunge to the floor.

It's too late. That kryptonite is giving off huge amounts of radiation. I can't move. The Kryptonite is too strong.

You writhe on the floor, completely helpless.

THE END

Answers

2

BRAINIAC IS BACK ON EARTH

3

12

FORTRESS

13

14

KRYPTONITE

G	R	E	E	N
H	O	M	E	I
K	C	R	Y	G
P	K	T	O	H
N	I	T	E	T

16

STOP ZOD

22

FIGHT ZOD

24

UNDERGROUND

29

VIDEO

32

GO BACK TO EARTH

C	G	O	B	M
L	A	O	C	E
A	K	R	T	E
R	O	B	O	T
K	O	I	E	S
A	R	T	T	H

34

HEAT VISION

39

SUPER-BREATH

40

49

GO TO PARIS

54

PEACE CONFERENCE

56

OTHER

57

58

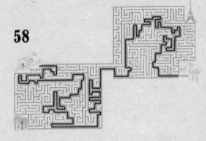

59

ZOD

Z	O	X		F
A	I	R		I
H	E	A		T
F	L	Y		D

Congratulations! You've saved the world from danger by following the path: 32, 53, 37, 47, 34, 30, 49, 31, 48, 41, 56, 23, 21, 9, 59, 40, 50, 16, 38, 7, 22, 5, 44, 24, 57, 51, 33, 2, 43, 4, 14, 46, 3, 35, 20, 11, 39, 12, 17, 52, 42, 13, 54, 19, 10